The Strange Story of the Man Who Murdered Time

Steve Wiley

Also by Steve Wiley

The Fairytale Chicago of Francesca Finnegan

The Curious Case of the Village in the Moonlight

A Beard Tangled in Dreams: The True Story of Rip Van Winkle

The Imagined Homecoming of Icarus Isakov

Copyright © 2026 by Lavender Line Press

All rights reserved. No part of this publication may be reproduced, distributed, or transmitted in any form or by any means, including photocopying, recording, or other electronic or mechanical methods, without the prior written permission of the publisher, except in the case of brief quotations embodied in critical reviews and certain other non-commercial uses permitted by copyright law. For permission requests, write to the publisher, addressed at the email below.

Lavenderlinepress@gmail.com

Ordering Information:

Quantity sales. Special discounts are available on quantity purchases by bookstores, corporations, associations, and others. For details, contact the publisher at the email address above.

Orders by U.S. trade bookstores and wholesalers may also order directly from Ingram Spark.

ISBN: 978-1-7353046-9-4

Part One

The Start of Time

The Village of Never Was

Once upon a time, there was no time. At least, not in one peculiar village.

The village did not drift with those doom-currents down the river of time. It sat safe and sound on the water's edge. Because of its location, the village was not behind the times or ahead of the times. It was entirely outside of time.

The precise location of the village was said to be secret, but stories give hints. They speak of lands outside of time, accessed through wardrobes and rabbit holes. "Second star to the right, straight on till morning," says the time-defying Peter Pan.

One ancient tale relates the location of our village and properties of time within it. It is a Celtic legend, which names the place Tír na nÓg, or Land of the Young. In the tale, an ordinary man falls in love with a princess from Tír na nÓg. She brings him to that timeless land, riding with him over the sea on a white horse. The lovers live in Tír na nÓg for what seems like a few short years. Eventually, the man grows homesick and asks to return to the ordinary world. The princess agrees to ride him back, but warns him not to dismount from the horse. Upon his return, the man finds that centuries have somehow passed. He touches the ground, time catches up with him, and he quickly turns to bone-dust.

Townsfolk did not refer to our quaint and clockless village as Tír na nÓg, Neverland, or Narnia. Instead, they referred to it quite plainly as the "Village." We shall refer to it in more precise terms, as the "Village of Never Was."

Having no time gave the village a uniquely enchanted quality. Without time, nothing ever ended. Lives were never lost. Seasons never passed. Games were never decided. Songs had no final chord. Stories had no end.

Our scientifically-minded readers may find it hard to believe that a village (or anything else) could exist without the property of time. It can. A village in itself does not require time to exist. It is true that our current understanding of physics requires time for anything to happen in the village, but that theory is now the subject of some debate. Quantum mechanics have challenged ideas related to the passage of time and the necessity of it for events to unfold. One recent, eerie experiment showed what amounted to cars exiting a tunnel in the time before having entering it[1].

Timelessness and quantum physics aside, the village was rather ordinary. It looked no different from other storybook villages. It was nestled within a little valley split by a slender, fast-flowing river. It was woven with narrow, cobblestone streets. Families lived in thatched, flower-adorned cottages. The rolling hills that surrounded the village were dotted with farms. Beyond the hills was one of those immense, fairytale forests. An uncrossable sea lay beyond that.

There were no more than a few hundred inhabitants of the village. There were farmers. There were tradesman and craftsman. There was a tailor, tavern-keeper, baker and

---

1. https://www.scientificamerican.com/article/evidence-of-negative-time-found-in-quantum-physics-experiment/

blacksmith. The social gathering place was the village tavern. The spiritual gathering place was the fairy tree.

Without the bother of time, villagers lived lives of blissful tranquility. They didn't rush. They walked. They didn't work to exhaustion or to deadlines. They rested. They didn't deliberate and scheme. They breathed. They didn't look down at ledgers of accounts. They looked up at constellations of stars.

Without the passage of time, there was no progress in the village. There was no electricity. There were no telephones or televisions. There were no engines. Men were used to plow fields instead of motors. There was no machine more modern than the windmill.

The village was primitive and better off because of it. Villagers were not isolated. They spoke to and saw one another. They were not compulsive consumers. They were not in debt. They were slow dancers and romancers. They were drinkers and thinkers. They were made happy not by things, but by one another.

Like many small towns, that one was immune to change. No one left the town. No one entered the town. Everyone knew everyone in the town. Folks went about their lives without the authority of time. They lived for the day, for eternity. They fell in love and never fell out of it.

But all of that was about to change.

The town watchman was the first to notice the change. He was watching for it. His name was Silas. He was like his name —simple and from another era. There was also an adventurous side to him, one that had until that fateful night been dormant.

Silas wandered the village streets after dark like a wayfaring spirit. He was like a wayfarer in that he had no real purpose, there never being any danger to the village. He was like a spirit in appearance, always dressed in a white tunic with a hood so immense it made him look like the Ghost of Christmas Yet to Come. "Yet to Come" had until then never come. It would soon arrive, along with yesterday.

What does a watchman watch in a town without trouble, or time? Dreams, mostly.

Dreams were everywhere in the Village of Never Was. The borderland between the wakeful and dreamful worlds there was faint, because neither of those realms adhered to the laws of time. There was never an unrealized dream in the village. Dreams there didn't just come true, they were true.

Each evening, after the lamplighter had done his duty, when the villagers had settled into their homes for supper and song, Silas began his nightly stroll. He watched as small-town dreams scurried from open windows like children off to some midnight tryst.

Silas watched the dreams of the townsfolk on their midnight gallivants. The dreams of drinkers were indistinguishable from their waking selves. They proceeded to the tavern. Some nights the watchman joined them. The dreams of lovers found someone else to love. Why shouldn't they? One night, Silas kissed the milkman's dreaming wife in the light of a full moon. His milk was spoiled rotten the next day.

Some dreamers simply roamed the streets, looking for something they could never seem to find, not knowing what that something even was. Silas often wandered with them. He felt like he was looking for something which had yet to be found, something destined to change his life.

The lucid dreamers acknowledged the watchman. Lucid dreamers are a rare breed. They are the privileged few who know they are dreaming. Most have no idea.

"Silas, if I didn't know any better I'd say you were a dream," the lucid would say.

At night, Silas did resemble a dream. He looked like something conjured from Carl Jung himself.

"Dream for me a pink moon," Silas would say back. "So that I might see better."

A pink moon would rise. The village was doused with dreams. Houses swayed here and there in the wind. Stars dangled in that same wind like string lights. Trees came to life, wandering the lanes in stupendous strides. The lanes themselves slithered as if alive, their cobblestone swirled and smeared in certain places, like a Van Gogh painting come to life.

There were less dreams about that night. That was the first sign something was not quite right. There were other, less noticeable signs. An oak leaf faded with the first hints of autumn. There was a noticeable chill in the air. A once deathless butterfly died.

Time had finally arrived.

It crept into the village like a band of thieves in the night. They made no sound. They gave no warning. Invisible yet all-powerful, they would steal nothing at once, yet everything forever.

Time cast its eternal spell at midnight. That is to say, it created midnight. Few of the townsfolk were awake to notice it. Silas saw it happen. So did an owl. He was a night owl. He liked to sit and sway in the topmost branches of a pine, overlooking the picturesque village as it slept.

Until then, there had been nothing unusual about the night. The owl had watched as Silas watched, and wandered. Each smelled the supper-smoke breathing from chimneys.

They saw the lights dim in each of the windows. They watched the cats chase the mice through the emptied streets. Then it happened.

A street lamp burned out.

Anywhere else, such an occurrence would hardly have been worth noticing. There, it was more than noticeable. It was extraordinary. Fires did not fade in the Village of Never Was. They would fade thereafter, as would everything else. Time has a tendency to do that.

The owl heard the lamp go dark. It made an ominous clicking noise, like the tick of a clock. The tick rent the night like thunder. The owl flew near to the odd lamp, perching a safe distance away. The owl stared suspiciously at it, wondering what black magic had smothered the thing.

Silas encountered the quenched lamp on his nightly stroll. He stood there awestruck, staring up, wondering if the dreams of that evening weren't playing tricks on his eyes. When it became clear the flame had truly died, he wondered how such a thing could have happened and what to do about it. The hour was late. He was no lamplighter. The lamplighter was asleep.

There was nothing for the watchman to do but watch. Silas stared at the street lamp, waiting from some sudden re-igniting of the fire. Of course, nothing of the sort would happen. Time would simply pass. Time had never passed Silas, or anyone else in the village. The owl could feel it travel by him. It felt like wind in the trees—hardly noticeable, yet all around.

Of Time

The second villager to notice time was the poet. The poet had been awake with the owl and watchman when time first arrived. He was often awake at night, being one of those occasional insomniacs like Dickens or Proust, who were at their most creative in the middle of the night.

The poet was writing when it happened. Being a poet in that peculiar village was a blessing and a curse. He was always writing poems, which for a poet was no doubt wonderful. The problem was he'd not finished a single one. Nothing ever finished in the Village of Never Was.

He sat writing in the lantern-light, face creased with sleep. He looked out the window, up to the stars for inspiration. The stars stared back at him without a word. Then, something happened which had never happened before. He wrote, and wrote some more. He wrote until he finished a poem.

It was no Shakespeare, but it was something—a limerick, to be exact.

There was once a poet without a shred of verse
The village he lived in was something of a curse

Until one morning at the break of day
The poet finished what he had to say
And wrote thereafter until his turn in the hearse

The poet was in a state of disbelief. He held the poem nearer to the light, examining it as if it were some precious gemstone. He read and re-read it. He had to be certain it had actually been finished. Was he dreaming? No. It had happened. The poet had finally written a poem.

It was the triumph of his life. Naturally, he began writing again. He wrote feverishly. He wrote with reckless abandon. He wrote like a writer. He wrote and wrote and wrote.

The poet wrote no less than a dozen poems before a single sunbeam peaked over the horizon. Mostly limericks. None are worthy of republication here. That wasn't important. What was important was that he'd finished. He had to.

Because for the first time, he was running out of time.

The letter carrier noticed time later that morning. Like any good letter carrier, he was awake before much of the town. While the poet was writing, he was sorting and packing the mail, preparing for his route.

The letter carrier in that peculiar place was, of course, no ordinary deliverer of bills and thank-you cards. In the Village of Never Was, the letter carrier delivered letters that were never sent. The absence of time only allowed for the origination and transport of such correspondence.

The letter carrier delivered all those love letters never sent. There were invitations to never-happened weddings. There were postcards from destinations never traveled, from imagined adventurers. There were forgotten reconnections to forgotten friends.

So, townsfolk looked forward to the mail. They looked forward to it the way we all used to. The letter carrier was a mystery-keeper. In his satchel were secrets. Sadly, those times have passed. Few remain on the lookout for that handwritten letter. Fewer are left with the spirit to write them.

The letter carrier took his usual path through the village that morning. At first, nothing seemed out of the ordinary. The veil of night had lifted. The last stubborn stars faded. The chirping birds declared it a new day. The letter carrier paid the birds and brightening sky no mind. He had a job to do.

He delivered letters with all those familiar pleasantries.

"And a good morning to you too missus."

"Never was a finer day sir."

"A grand afternoon. Just grand."

The letter carrier was everyone's friend. Friend was once in the job description of a letter carrier. Deliverer of mail and courteous, inconsequential conversation.

The letter carrier was nearing the end of his route when he uncovered an unusual letter. It was an apology letter. There were no such thing as apologies in the Village of Never Was, because there was no such thing as regret. There was no such thing as regret because there was no such thing as time. Or, was there?

The letter carrier delivered the letter with a shake of his head, knowing in his heart of hearts time had arrived.

"Nothing good will come of this," he said to himself.

There were two lovers in the village who, without the bother of time, never fell out of love.

They met in secret every afternoon. Their trysting place was a grove of outcast oaks from the fairytale forest on the outskirts of town. There, the lovers would do all those things lovers do, over and over, day in and day out. Time did not bore the routine.

She noticed time on that day where it is most noticeable—the mirror. She was preparing for their meeting when she first saw it. In truth, no preparation was needed. She was flawless. She was dreamt. She was young, as we all once were.

At first, she thought it was an errant piece of gray string. It fell from her hair as she ran her fingers through it. She held it up, carefully examining it. There could be no doubt. It was a strand of her hair.

She inspected the rest of her head, discovering several more gray hairs. Then she found a patch of white roots and nearly fainted. She raced from her house through the streets and over the hills to the grove, as though she might outrun time itself.

He saw her frolicking across the meadow the way she always did. But, she was not alone. No, she brought something with her. Time. He could sense it. It wasn't within the hair that he noticed. It was within the kiss.

Yes, the kiss itself ultimately gave time away. Prior to that afternoon, every kiss they exchanged was one of unequaled power. Each one was every bit as potent as a first kiss. That is what every kiss is like without the intrusion of time. Time spoils kisses like it spoils bread.

The kiss that day was less potent, because it was a second kiss. It was the first second kiss the lovers ever had. A second kiss is wonderful, but not as wonderful as a first kiss. Each kiss is a little less important than the last. The diminishing strength of kisses remains to this day an indisputable law of the universe. This effect is quite noticeable, and was noticed that day.

There was something else that gave time away. It was her dress. It was a seemingly simple, robin egg blue sun dress. But in that village there was no such thing as a simple anything. Without the influence of time, even dresses were different.

The cloth did not thin or lose shape. The fabric did not fray or tear. Dresses remained unchanged.

There was something different about her dress that day. He watched it wave in the wind with suspicion. He could tell there was something different about it. The lovers embraced how they always did. Only when she drew back did he see it.

The dress had faded. There was an unmistakable patch of sun-stained ivory near the nipple.

"What is that?" he asked.

She was terrified, thinking he'd found a gray hair.

"What's what?" she asked back.

"That," he pointed to the dress.

They studied the imperfection, but not for long. They agreed the dress was better off anyway, and it soon was. Time passed them by that day, but they paid it no more attention.

Across town lay the fisherman. Yes, lay. Most fishermen sit or stand. Not this one. This fisherman never caught a fish. Why not lay down?

Not that catching fish is only the point of fishing. The point is also to relax, and relax our fisherman did. He lay against a tree, the wind composing riverside lullabies. Shadows of tree branches danced heavily upon his eyelids. He propped up his pole, closed his eyes, and was soon fast asleep.

The fisherman dreamt. In that other world, he actually caught fish. The fish he caught there were all a silvery trout. He pet their scales. He gutted them. He tasted their flesh. They tasted of nothing, because they weren't real. If only he could catch a real fish!

Then, he did.

The fisherman was startled awake by his pole, which jerked

forward from behind him. It thumped him on the head as if to say, "Wake up! You've caught something!"

He'd had nibbles before, but never a hook. The fish was tugging. The fisherman was unused to such tugging. His heart beat faster with each new tug. He pulled back, reeling in the catch as quick as he might. He reeled and reeled. He reeled like Captain Ahab.

It was no Moby Dick that he caught, but a simple, silver fish. It looked like all those he'd caught in dreams. Indeed, he thought he was dreaming. It was the flopping that convinced him he wasn't. The fisherman examined the fish for some time. It was more valuable to him than any treasure. He'd been fishing for that fish since the inception.

After he'd thoroughly inspected the fish, he placed it in his satchel and cast his line back into the blue yonder. He must catch another and it seemed to him that he would. Something was different. Something had changed. Something had allowed change.

Of course, that something was time. It ran like that river he fished. It ran and ran.

Later that day, two villagers played chess under the sprawling shade of an immense willow. Until that day, the game had been never-ending. In fact, it had been played for so long, neither of the players could remember when it had started.

Normally, the game was uneventful. A few pawns were captured, only to reappear the next day. A knight or rook might fall. Rarely a bishop. The queens were untouchable. The kings were immortal. The pair played the day away, and again the next day, without conclusion.

That day, the game was eventful. It was so eventful that it was over in less than two minutes.

It started with a blunder by White, who had exposed their king to an unblocked attack by the opposing queen. She obliged. In just two moves, White was checkmated. Such a sequence is called a "fool's mate." It is the fastest mate possible.

"Checkmate?" each player wondered at the same time.

An ending to the game was surprising, to say the least. The speed with which it ended was astonishing. The pair studied the board together for the rest of the afternoon, trying to work out if it were truly the end of the game. When they'd finally agreed that the game was indeed over, something else incredible happened.

A leaf fell from the willow.

There could be no mistaking the matter. Time had arrived.

Change came with the arrival of time. The signs were everywhere. Once bright roses paled, as if sickened. Faces wrinkled and reddened in the sun. Aged, weathered mortar dislodged stones from homes and hearths. Some even suspected the days were getting shorter and colder. Summer seemed to be withering.

The once eternal village now felt temporary. So did the villagers.

There was no clearer evidence for the passage of time than the newcomer. Until then, there was no such thing as a newcomer. The mysterious man was the first visitor to the town in forever. Before him no one had arrived and no one had left.

The newcomer was the talk of the town. Who was he? Where had he come from? What was his business? Was it he who had set the cosmic clock spinning?

Allow us to look in on the village tavern, where such matters were discussed.

The Tavern With No Name

The nameless tavern sat upon a lonely hill on the outskirts of town. A stream surrounded the base of the hill like a magical moat to defend from the incursion of time. On top of the hill, above the shadowy, fairytale forest beyond, candlelit windows shone like cheerful beacons.

A quaint, two-story red brick cottage, one might've mistaken it for an ordinary house, were it not for the plaque above the door. The plaque swung gently in the wind, peddling a frothing mug of hops and barley. Strings of thick ivy bordered the front door like decorative trim.

The tavern was as timeless as the rest of the town. The taps never ran dry. Tabs were never settled. Drinkers drank with an unquenchable thirst. They drank without consequence. They were served by a friendly barkeep. He was as jolly a spirit as those he poured.

The tavern was busier than usual that evening. There was much to discuss. The passing of time had not gone unnoticed. The fireplace crackled and popped with a new scent, as though it might not burn forever. Drinkers huddled around it in conversation.

"Today was a wonderful day," announced the poet.

"You mean a wonderless day," said the lamplighter. "Did you not hear? The flame of a street lamp was tragically vanquished."

"Not only that," said the farmer. "The sun set earlier than usual. I swear it!"

"Yes," added the blacksmith. "The breeze blew cool enough to chill the forge. Odd."

The eternal summer was at an end. It passed quickly. Time had catching up to do in that village. Soon, it would be the first autumn in forever.

"There is also the matter of this newcomer," said the lamplighter. "They say he has traveled from faraway lands. They say he is a philosopher."

The tavern was anxious. The barkeep could sense it.

"Tell us poet, what was so wonderful about this day?" the barkeep asked.

The poet stood upon his chair and cleared his throat. The tavern quieted.

"I have written a poem!"

The whole tavern gasped. The farmer spat out his beer. The cobbler fell from his stool, as if struck by lightning.

"Never!" a skeptic shouted.

The poet held up a scrap of paper as proof, then read aloud.

There was a nameless old tavern upon a hill
Where drinkers drank and time stood still
One night before the tipsy herd
A poet rose and spoke his word
Time had passed and passes there still

The tavern was still and silent as an old photograph. They all wondered what such a thing could mean. The completion of the poem was a sign of change. Time was the agent of that change. Had it begun to pass?

Time was known in the village, but not discussed. The word was avoided. Time was thought to be the scourge of some distant land. It was a faraway, fabled dragon of no real concern.

"He was bound to finish a poem eventually," someone said.

"Are we certain it is complete?" said another. "That was quite short."

"Indeed it was!"

All agreed with a collective sigh of relief that the poem was too short to be complete. Conversations of ordinary village happenings resumed. Drinkers returned to the bar. For a moment, all was back to normal.

"Ahem, your attention sirs!" the poet clapped his hands. "I assure you this poem is finished. It is a *limerick*. Such a poem is required by the laws of verse to be a mere five lines."

The tavern quieted again. None had any earthly idea what a limerick was. It sounded credible.

"I have finished more poems," the poet continued, "And would be happy to recite them..."

"No, no!" they all shouted. That was a tavern, not a literary salon.

There could be no arguing the fact the poem was finished, and probably many more after it. What did it mean? They were drinking and speculating as to how such a thing could happen, when Silas walked in. He often stopped in for a libation during his nightly watch.

Silas sat at his usual barstool. He signaled his usual drink, which was forever on tap. The barkeep began filling the glass with that beguiling brew, when something happened that had never happened before. Something unimaginable.

The tap ran dry.

Everyone saw it happen. The normal fizzing and flowing changed to a hissing and sputtering. The death rattle of that barrel of beer silenced the whole tavern. The mortified barkeep served the mortified Silas a half-full glass.

The drinkers sat staring in disbelief. They spoke in whispers. They drank slowly and mindfully, relishing the last of the drink for the first time in forever. The barkeep cleaned the bar surface nervously, as if nothing were wrong. The fire burned low. It never burned low.

Of course, the tap never went dry in the tavern with no name, in the Village of Never Was. Going dry meant to be forever finished, like the poem. Nothing ever finished in that town. Time had arrived. There was no doubt of that.

Time had passed and passes there still

The Philosopher

One summery afternoon, not long after the tap went dry, the townsfolk converged upon the village green. They came for the newcomer. The barkeep was right. He was a philosopher. Philosophers answer questions. The villagers had questions.

The philosopher waited for them under the fairy tree. He smoked a corncob pipe whose chamber was so enormous it looked more like a mug for drinking than a pipe for smoking. Still, few noticed the pipe. It was the man's age they were amazed by. He was *aged*.

Time had clearly passed him by. He looked like time, like a grandfather clock. He stood tall and square-shouldered with a pale beard that blew back and forth in the wind like a pendulum.

The villagers were also amazed by the fairy tree. It was an enormous maple. Its leaves had suddenly changed from their eternal green to a fiery orange-red. The villagers were mesmerized by the tree in the same way you or I would be, had the sun one day decided to turn from yellow to purple with no explanation whatsoever.

Silas was there, staring curiously along with everyone else. He was also afraid. The sight of the newcomer alone was distressing, not to mention the bewitched fairy tree. Here was a poor soul from that faraway land where the scourge of time reigned. Here was a victim.

Silas asked himself the same question the young always ask themselves when encountering the old.

"Will I someday be old?"

After which, he thought what the young always think.

"I refuse to ever be so old."

Many who answer the question in this seemingly naïve way are not naïve at all. Some do in fact die young, remaining so forever. Most of course are wrong and do indeed grow old. Still, in that moment the future was not real. Not for Silas. It was an idea. So, his refusal to accept it was enough.

The villagers circled around the fairy tree and the questioning began.

"Who are you and where are you from?" were the first questions. Remember, he was the first visitor to the town in forever.

"I am a philosopher from a faraway kingdom, beyond the uncrossable sea."

"What is a philosopher, exactly?" someone asked. It was an honest question. Few small towns have full-time philosophers. Philosophizing in small towns is a hobby, not a profession.

"A philosopher is one who has been initiated into the secrets of the universe."

The villagers pretended that made sense and went on questioning.

"If the sea is uncrossable, how did you cross it?" was the next logical question.

"I did not cross it. I went around it. The way was long."

"Why have you come from so far?"

"Why not? This is a magnificent land. Almost magical. I understand it was untouched by time, until recently."

The villagers fell quiet at the mention of time.

"It is true," continued the philosopher. "Time is here. Have you not seen it?"

"Where?" Silas asked. "What does time look like?"

"Time takes many forms. It is a thief. It is a fast and forever-flowing river. Time flies. It is a winged serpent. It is an all-consuming dragon. Time is a devourer of life. It will consume you. It will swallow this little village, and the rest of the world with it."

The villagers gasped. They took the philosopher at his word. They looked to the hills in the distance for some sign of the dragon. The looked at each other, wondering if the thief of time was in their midst. They backed away from the river, lest flowing time consume them.

"We must seek out time and vanquish it!" said the miller. "How do we slay time?"

"I've not seen time slain in the way you mean," said the philosopher between long, wizardly puffs of his immense pipe. "Which isn't to say it can't be done."

"Where does one find time, to end it once and for all?" asked Silas.

"Ask not where to find time, but what to do with that sliver of it that you've been granted. It is all you have."

"How much time do we have, exactly?"

"A lifetime."

"How long is a lifetime?"

"Relatively short."

"How short?"

The philosopher removed the pipe from his mouth. The

villagers fell silent. Here was perhaps the most important question. When would time come for them?

"If all time were a vast sea, the meaning and span of your lives would be an imperceptibly tiny drop of water. Nothing you do matters. In good time, you will have forgotten everything and you yourself will have been forgotten. Your bones will turn to dust. The bones of your descendants will turn to dust. You will be no one and nowhere, as will I. Time will see to it."

"No! No!" shouts of denial sounded from the crowd.

"What shall we do with the time we have?" someone asked.

To this the philosopher responded immediately.

"Why, set forth on an adventure."

"What adventure?"

"The adventure of a lifetime."

The crowd fell silent. Adventure? What did he mean?

Adventures were feared or frowned upon by most in that village, but not by Silas. In fact, adventure sounded like the very thing he had been watching for all those long, lonely nights. Silas thought to himself he ought to go on an adventure—an adventure to vanquish time.

A Timely Conspiracy

Time passed. The philosopher left, never to return. The days grew darker and colder. Winter was at hand—the first one for the oblivious villagers. Some wondered if the world was ending. That is what winter feels like for those unaccustomed to it.

One unforgiving night, a cruel cold left the village streets desolate. Townsfolk took refuge in the tavern. The fire would warm them. The drinks would drown their sorrows. The friends would cure their weariness. There is no better hideaway from a winter's night than a tavern.

The tavern was busy that night. The fire roared. Drinkers roared along with it. They told tales of toil and time. They drank to help the storytelling. They drank to help the story-listening. They drank and drank. Some forgot about the scourge of seconds altogether.

One group sat around a corner table in a more serious conversation. They were conspirators against time. They intended to rid the village of it, once and for all. Silas was among them.

"All instruments to recognize and record time should be

destroyed," said the blacksmith. "My forge can be used for that purpose."

"And all means of tracking time should be banned," said the carpenter.

"And any found guilty of keeping time banished," added the tailor.

The wind thrashed against the windows, as if in disagreement. A breath of cold snuck through a crack in the wall, causing the candle fire to dance. The conspiracy might not stop time, but they might ignore it or hide from it awhile.

"Would it not be better to seek out time and destroy it?" said Silas. "Surely, that would be better than hiding from it."

The conspirators sipped their drinks nervously. None had ever ventured far from the village and none were willing. There was no telling what lurked in the woods and beyond. Stories told of brigands, ghosts, and worse.

"It seems to me time must have some place of origin," Silas continued. "The philosopher said it was a thief. Perhaps there are thieves deep in the forest who have set time against us."

"The philosopher spoke also of a dragon," said the poet. "It may be that the slaying of such a serpent would stop time."

"He spoke also of a river," said Silas. "Something about time running with it, or along it."

"Yes. Perhaps we should dam the river," said the blacksmith.

"The fisherman will not be happy."

"Nor the miller."

"Leave the river alone," said Silas. "Better to follow the river into the woods. Its source may be time itself."

The suggestion that someone leave the village again quieted the conspirators. They sipped their drinks and looked out the window. The wind howled loud as ever, warning of the coming storm. A cold drizzle had begun.

"I was on watch when time slipped by," said Silas. "I should go."

"You *are* the watchman," the poet agreed.

"I will follow the river into the forest," explained Silas. "I will stop the river if it flows with time. I will seek out those thieves of time and steal it all back. If there is a dragon spewing forth time, I will find and slay the serpent. I will stop time."

The conspirators shook their heads in agreement, thinking him crazy. None volunteered to go with him. Instead, they ordered more drinks, then more after that. The conspiracy changed from the conquest of time to the conquest of the bar.

The concern of time fell from their minds. It always does in taverns, which is why so few have clocks. Still, time is persistent. It will remind everyone of its existence eventually. That night, it reminded them from outside.

"Look at that!" someone yelled, pointing to the window. They all looked outside.

The rain had turned to snow and was falling in white, doughy gobs. No one would leave the tavern until very late into the night. The first snow was falling too hard and looked too beautiful from the inside. The passing of time was worth watching on that night. It often is.

Part Two

The Pursuit of Time

Time is a River

Most spend their lives ignoring time, pretending it isn't after them. They conceal time with makeup in the mirror and go about their day. Others are more conscious of time. They hide from it. They cling to it in memories. The ambitious run from time. They beat it to the office, to the altar, to the next big thing. They think if they keep beating it, they will beat it forever.

Some have sought remedies for time. The conquistador Juan Ponce de Leon spent years searching for the fountain of youth in what is now Florida. A poisoned arrow found him first. Nowadays, entrepreneurs seek a cure for time with pills and gadgets.

Few like Silas actually pursue time. Naturally, most in the village thought him insane. The letter carrier was the only one awake to see him off on that misty morning.

"Farewell letter carrier. I am off on an adventure, in pursuit of time."

"Best of luck to you watchman, or should I say huntsman? That is what you've become."

"It seems so," Silas smiled, very much liking his new title.

"If you do find time, ask him what he has done with the summer. Perhaps you can arrange for the delivery of some semblance of sunshine?"

"Perhaps."

Silas waved goodbye and followed the river out of town. It slithered through the hills before entering the fairytale forest. He stopped at a meadow which bordered the woods and wilderness beyond. The trees swayed, wailing a warning in the wind. He turned and watched the town once more, before leaving it watchless.

A word about the woods before we enter. As its nickname implied, the forest was one of those mystical ones spoken of only in fairy stories. Fairytale forests are dense. That particular one was an enclosure. Once inside, there was no proof of outside. The only evidence of anything other than the forest was the occasional patch of sun or starlight, but those appeared less and less as one made their way deeper into the heart of the forest. In the hidden chambers of that heart lurked strange sights.

Silas followed a narrow path along the river into the forest. The trees were thick and crowded, with gnarled and gnomish faces. They stared amazedly at Silas as he passed them by, wondering whatever he was doing in those parts. Villagers hardly ever ventured into the forest. The moment the watchman entered the woods he felt less a like watcher than one who is being watched.

He followed the river, always on the lookout for time. He thought he saw it once or twice, always at night as he camped on the riverside. The waters whispered for him to wake up. He did and though he couldn't see anything, he often felt a strange presence in the river.

Silas saw other peculiar sights in those woods—sights which reminded him of dreams from before the incursion of time. There were gatherings of fairies within glades on moonlit nights. Silas watched from the trees with other creatures of the forest, as though it were a play. There were ghosts. Silas saw the apparition of a woman parading through the trees with a train of dwarves in tow. She sang a sad song, her voice rising and falling with the wind.

Silas watched these strange occurrences from a safe distance. He did not stray from the river into the woods. The river was the only known path into and out of that labyrinth. The forest seemed to have no end, as did the river.

Silas journeyed on. The days grew so short they seemed like half-mornings. The nights felt like weeks. He grew tired and hopeless. He longed for home. He felt he was on a fool's errand. Fairytale forests cast such spells, disillusioning hunters and heroes.

Then, on one of those cold and hopeless eternal nights, Silas was certain he saw time. It was in the river. He couldn't sleep and so peered into the waters for some sign of the past or future, or anything at all. There was a faint glimmer, then a whisper. It whispered for him to come nearer. He did.

Looking into the river, he saw a flurry of tiny lights. They were just below the surface. It looked as if the lights from the stars reflecting on the water had broken into hundreds of little fish and gone fluttering in all directions.

Silas's first reaction was to leap into the river at what he presumed was time, without much thought to the consequences. In the seconds between when he left the ground and hit the water, he did have one thought. The thought came too late—he couldn't swim.

His eyes opened wide under the water at the shock of the cold. He looked for the light of time. He saw it a few feet under him, glowing faintly. He sank toward it. Time was no bigger than a perch. He grabbed for it, but could never seem to reach it. It would allow him to get within arm's reach, then dart away, drawing him deeper and deeper, until he found himself at the bed of the river.

Standing on the muddy river bed, out of breath and nearly out of life, he felt as though time stood upon him. It pushed him down until his knees buckled below him into the earth, then down farther. It pushed him down until the river was gone. He felt as though he were falling through the air. Then, he felt no more.

Silas awoke on the banks of the river. The first thing he saw were the expressionless eyes of an otter. The otter, with the help of a muskrat, had saved him. They had been following him for some time, mostly out of curiosity. Humans were an oddity in those parts.

"Hello," said the otter. "What were you doing at the bottom of my river?"

"Good day," said Silas, as though he'd known many an otter. "I was in pursuit of time. I saw it, there in the river, under the starlight."

The otter stared at Silas, thinking him mad. Wild, woodland creatures have no sense or concept of time. They exist for today and today alone.

"Have you seen time in these parts?" asked Silas. "I intend to vanquish it, once and for all."

"I know nothing of time, though I know someone who may. Follow me."

Silas followed the otter as he scurried away from the river

into the woods. Morning sunbeams pierced the tree canopy. The pair followed an invisible trail, known only to the nose of the otter. It ran along narrow ravines, down through dark dells, up and over towering knolls which rose like citadels above the treetops. It wasn't long before Silas felt hopelessly lost.

They eventually came upon a glade. An enormous tree stood in the middle with animals of all kinds hidden among the roots and perched within the branches. There were moles, foxes, hawks, even a black bear. They stopped and stared as the otter brought Silas forth.

They were greeted by a pair of jack o-lantern eyes high in the tree.

"Hooooooooooooooooot," hooted the owl.

Howls, barks, and growls sounded from the rest of the animals before they quieted. It seemed to Silas they were conversing in their own language.

"This man is in pursuit of something called 'time' Master Owl. Can you help him catch it?"

The owl flew to a lower branch, peering Silas over with those pumpkin eyes.

"Time, eh?" asked the owl. "What's the worry with time? Hoot!"

The hoot was like a shrill declaration of truth.

"Time lays waste to my village," said Silas. "It must be stopped. Things should be as they once were, with no time at all."

"Is it your hope that without time, things may never change? That you may not change? You wish for you and your village to remain unchanged forever?"

"Yes."

The owl gave no immediate response. He sat perched on his branch in contemplation. The rest of the animals whispered to one another in confusion. Forever was not a concept they understood. The present was all that existed for them.

"You are chasing a ghost," explained the owl. "There is no tomorrow, not for we creatures of the wood. The young otter does not worry about someday being an old otter. The bear may sense a change of seasons, but he does not deny them. The fox hunts with no care for the past or future. He eats when he is hungry. He sleeps when he is tired. Hoot!"

Silas was no woodland creature. Time felt as real as the weather. It altered his mood. It gave him hope. It worried him. Sometimes, it scared him.

"The time that you pursue is a mere thought," said the owl, as if reading his mind. "You torture yourself with remembrances of an unreachable past and a future that has yet to be. These are ideas. Ideas are not real."

"What *is* time, if not something real?" asked Silas.

"Time is now. This moment. And it seems to this owl that you are wasting it."

"Is there not a thievish nature to time?" asked Silas. "Tales tell of time as a swindler of souls."

"Otter, escort this man to the den of thieves. Perhaps they can aid him in his pursuit of time. Hoot!"

Time is a Thief

The otter led Silas away. They wound their way through the watchful woods to the den of thieves. The path was hopelessly meandering. Silas felt as though they were walking in circles. He felt he was forever lost. Still, he traveled on in search of time.

About the thieves. That particular band of thieves was not engaged in run-of-the-mill thievery. They were not concerned with precious gems. They did not pick pockets or rob banks. Those thieves stole only the most elusive of treasures.

They stole wishes from the depths of wishing wells. They stole dreams and made them their own. They stole hearts, minds, even souls. They stole cleverness from foxes. They stole guiltlessness from children. They stole shade from trees and the wind in their boughs, to keep cool on the hottest of summer nights. They stole the stardust from the sky. They tried for the stars, but could never seem to catch them.

The thieves lived in a secret and distant corner of the forest. Such was the way of outlaws in those days. Robin Hood and his merry men lived in the haunted heart of Sherwood. The Forty Thieves of Ali Baba kept their den in a secret cavern. These hidden enclaves were free from the laws and subjugation of man.

This particular den was so dense with trees it looked more fort than forest. The rain did not fall there. The sun did not shine. Still, there was sunlight. The youngest of thieves stole it from the groves and meadows where they played. They stored the sunlight in jars that they strung from the trees like lanterns.

The otter led Silas to the border of the den.

"This place reeks of thievery," said the otter. "They don't take kindly to otters. Might steal the fur off my back. Go on ahead sir, toward the lights and larceny."

"Thank you, otter," said Silas. "For saving me and showing me the way."

But the otter was already gone, having vanished into the trees.

Silas crept into the den, hand at the hilt of the small sword forged for him by the blacksmith. He was determined to find and slay that thief who was time. The den looked more like a quaint, forest hamlet than any haven of banditry. Huts were nestled high among the trees, connected by a network of bridges and ladders. There were straw cottages on the ground along the main thoroughfare.

The thieves did not look thievish. They looked more mischievous than villainous. They looked like Silas. He, like most men, had traces of banditry in his blood. The prince and the pickpocket are not so different as stories make them out to be.

Silas was surprised at the sight of women and children. There appeared to be whole extended families of thieves. It was the children who greeted him first.

"Welcome mister," said one boy, as he dug through Silas's pocket. "You lost?"

"I am."

"I'll show you the way," said the boy, who was joined by several other curious children. They showed him the way, stealing everything from him but the clothes on his back.

Silas was led to a great bonfire within a clearing just off the main road. Thieves drank and danced and dreamed stolen dreams around the fire. A pair of cackling whores swept Silas off his feet. Before he knew it he was drinking and dancing and dreaming right along with them.

Silas felt as though a spell had been cast on him. His senses dulled, as though he were an unwilling participant in some pilfered dream. He danced round and round in a heedless trance. He danced about as well as any watchman. That is to say, not well. He looked ridiculous. He looked more marionette than man. He had no control of his body. Who the puppeteer was Silas had no idea, but some sorcery had possessed him.

How long Silas spent twirling around the fire is hard to say. If one could recount minutes as they pass in a dream, some estimation might be possible. It was likely quite long, but the spell did finally fade with the fire.

They settled around the embers on seats of stumps and stone, singing and storytelling. They spoke of legendary heists, of treasures beyond measure. Silas told of his watching the village and questing in the forest. They asked him what he quested after and what brought him into their realm.

"I am looking for a thief," Silas declared.

"Nothing of the sort here!" they laughed. "What sort of thief do you seek? What does he look like?"

"I am looking for the thief that is time."

They laughed harder at that.

"Is time not a thief?" Silas asked.

"Time is the emperor of all thieves," they said. "There is nothing he cannot steal."

"I expected such a master thief to be here, among his own," said Silas.

"Awaken the elder," someone said. "She will have something to say on the matter. No one has more experience with time than her."

As they waited around the embers, Silas wondered what time of day it was. He'd lost track of it, being unable to see the sky through the canopy of leaves.

Soon an old crone was led to a seat by the fire. She was blind. She knew time. It had stolen everything from her except for a few remnants of life.

"Grandmother, our guest hunts time. He believes it to be a thief among us. What do you know of time? Can you help him capture it?"

"Time is not a thief," she said. "It is a thread."

The thieves listened intently. Perhaps time could be stolen after all.

"The thread of time binds us," she said. "It extends from yesterday to tomorrow. The thread is woven into a fabric that is stitched with lives."

"Where is the source of this thread?" asked Silas. "Every thread has a source. I had thought it flowed within the river, but was mistaken. It seems I was also mistaken in my believing this band of thieves had stolen time."

"When I was a girl, I wandered the woods at night. The trees slept. I crept upon them and stole their memories. Most of the memories were ordinary. The scent of spring. Summer rain. Undressing for autumn. The touch of first snow. But, there was one curious memory. I stole it from a great pine. In the memory, a thread was being pulled from the dress of a princess. The dress was said to be flecked with stars from the dawn of the time. The dress did not fade or blemish."

The Strange Story of the Man Who Murdered Time

The forest grew still as she told her tale. The trees listened as keenly as the thieves.

"She who wore the dress had lived a thousand lifetimes. For in wearing the dress of time, she had dominion over it. They say she was once the princess of a powerful woodland kingdom. The most skilled of sorcerers wove the dress for her as a gift."

The old woman's face changed. For a moment, she was young and beautiful again.

"The dress was the most cherished treasure of the kingdom. But where there is treasure, there are dragons. One lived in those parts. It sat perched high on the mountains, overlooking the kingdom. The dragon saw the princess in the unfading dress and desired it."

"One night, the princess stood alone on the castle ramparts studying the stars. She observed what at first looked like two newly appeared stars behaving strangely. The stars twirled and blinked erratically in the darkness, like a pair of faraway fireflies. They grew larger and climbed higher, as if they were the eyes of some soaring eagle. She watched until the lights were upon her, until it became clear what it was they were. When she realized what they were, her curiosity turned to dread. They were the smoldering eyes of the vast, golden-garnet dragon."

"The serpent stole her away to his mountain lair. The princess was never seen again, but she was heard. They say on the windiest of nights, her voice can be heard calling for help. She calls out forever and ever because while wearing the dress, she lives forever."

"Did no one try to save her?" asked Silas.

"Yes. The kingdom was filled with the noblest of knights. Whole armies ventured forth into the mountains to rescue her. None succeeded. Some were defeated by the mountains. Others by the dragon itself. Time passed. The kingdom withered away and died like all kingdoms before it. The princess faded from memory into legend, then to almost nothing at all."

The thieves listened for some plea from the mountains.

"Time," the elder looked at Silas. "Is in the threads of that dress."

~

A brief interlude from Silas and his peculiar pursuit of time. Let us return now to the village.

Time passed through the unwitting woods, by the flowers and foxes and fireflies. It passed by the farms and fields. It passed overhead, in the summer storms and through their tapestried sunsets. Time passed by the Village of Never Was.

For the villagers, time was a strange scourge. It afflicted each person differently. A lucky few were hardly bothered by it. Others were entirely overcome with it. Most were somewhat sickened by its passing. They complained of aches in their bones and fog in their brains.

Although time had arrived to the village all at once, it passed by villagers at different rates. Some found themselves very old, very soon. Others seemed not to age at all. The varying speed at which time passed for the villagers made sense. Time is subjective. It passes swiftly for some and slowly for others.

The poet remained young. He was one of those lucky few for whom time seemed not to pass, or to pass very slowly. He passed his days writing and roaming the hills on the outskirts of town. He passed his nights drinking and philosophizing in the tavern.

His remained a life of firsts. First poems. First loves. First lost loves. First fistfights. His days were filled with novelty and adventure. Time was of little concern to him. It passed so slow that at times he hardly believed in its existence. He loved life and could not imagine its end.

The letter carrier was not so lucky. He'd quickly become one of the oldest in town. Time had ravaged him. His once raven-black hair had turned a ghostly white. He was handsome no more, his face a maze of wrinkles and liver spots. His back had hunched. His body was frail.

More disturbing than his physical appearance was his mental state. He was losing his mind. He got lost on his daily route. He often delivered mail to the wrong house. No one dared complain. They pitied the old letter carrier. They wondered when time would finish him. They wondered when it would come for them.

"Where has the time gone?" the letter carrier often wondered to himself.

Where the time had gone was a more difficult question to answer than why it had gone so quickly. The letter carrier led a life of routine. Unlike the poet, there was hardly ever any newness to it. He woke, worked, and went to bed. His days were made of such structure and efficiency, they actually sped up. He often wanted them to. So, they did.

There was little worth remembering in his days of delivering the mail. So, he didn't remember them. This helped time to overtake him with such swiftness. If yesterday wasn't worth remembering, time seemed to have skipped it altogether.

Time passed slowly for the playful. The young at heart stayed young. Time passed swiftly for the serious. It made jokes of their solemnity and sincerity. Time laid waste to the lawyers. It ruined the bankers and businessman. Strangely, few of them seemed to notice or care.

Although time afflicted each individual differently, there was one unusual property of it that applied to all. With each passing day, it passed faster. One evening, the subject was contemplated in the tavern with no name. A tavern is the best place to ponder time, because there is an endless supply of it there. There are no deadlines or appointments. There is no rush. That is why taverns contain no clocks.

"I swear by the stars that yesterday was shorter than today," said the miller.

"And the day before yesterday was shorter than that," agreed the butcher.

"Here, here!" all agreed.

"Where does the time go?" the barkeep wondered, along with everyone else.

"Time is written into memory and filed away within all those secret compartments of the heart," lyricized the poet in a tone that was more factual than lyrical.

"Come again?" asked the farmer.

"He means time is gone. Once it goes it's gone," clarified the blacksmith. The blacksmith knew all too well that time was gone, never to return. More time had passed him by than most.

"Last call!" shouted the barkeep, the sole keeper of time in the place.

"Time is up, always up," groaned the drinkers.

"If the time were in any general direction," corrected the poet, "it would not be up. It would be behind you. Not for me. No. Time is always in front of me. Keep it in front of you, gentlemen. May it not pass you by without your knowing it."

The tavern slowly emptied. A sorrowful ballad played. Candles were blown out. Parting glasses were drunk. Oaths were taken. Promises made. Hands shaken. Hugs given. The drinkers made their way into the night with dizzy, drunken steps toward home.

The farmer followed a country lane, clear as morning in the moonlight. The lamplighter took to the fields. He was accustomed to a lonely jaunt under the stars. The blacksmith took a shortcut through the woods. He knew all the shortcuts, old as he was. The miller was so drunk he didn't know the way home. Luckily, his horse did.

The poet did not go straight home. He stopped at the wishing well. He stopped there not for a wish, but for a kiss. She waited for him there, sitting on the edge of that grimy, ages-old alter of dreams.

The poet claimed that kiss he'd come for on that and so many other nights before. And just like on those other nights, he eluded time. The crickets fell silent. The wind died. The stars stopped their shining. The moon stopped its sailing. All of time stopped, all at once. Such is the sorcery of a simple kiss.

Time is a Fabric

When we last left Silas, he'd been told of a mystical dress threaded with time itself. He set out again into the forest, determined to find some trace of the thread. Some of the more daring thieves ventured out after the dress as well. The thieves meant to steal and possess it. Silas meant to destroy it.

Of course, there was the matter of the dragon. A dragon is always a matter of concern. Silas was less concerned than he was inspired. He suddenly felt himself that valorous hero of so many tales. He was off to slay the serpent, to save the captive princess.

The old crone had nothing to say about where in the woods one might find the thread, or what it looked like. So, the watchman went the way one goes without any direction or destination. Forward. He found a trail into the trees and took it.

Like any fairytale forest, that one had perilous properties. Certain patches of trees did not emit a vapor of water and oxygen like ordinary trees. They emitted a haze, which when inhaled brought on dizziness and confusion. In that way, the forest was often inescapable.

The haze was a hardly noticeable mist. Silas strode through it without noticing. Soon, he forgot where he was. Then he forgot who he was. He wandered the forest with little of his mind left to do anything other than wander. His sense of self had dissipated to no more than the sensations of his feet on the forest floor. He was everything and nothing, all at once.

Silas walked and walked, undisturbed by thought. He was naked, uncritical attention. He felt free from the burden of himself, and whatever life he'd lived. He was a faceless, beingless being, staying to the strange path by some inexplicable force and feeling.

He traveled deeper into the forest. The deeper he delved, the more lost he became and the stranger he felt. He couldn't distinguish his hand from his foot, or his hair from the wind. He walked not on the ground but on the air, up through the treetops and into the stars. Then back again.

He saw from the eyes of the forest and its inhabitants. He was a barn owl perched high on a treetop, looking over the endless green expanse of other treetops. He was an acorn, blown free from its branch, rolling down a rocky slope and into a rabbit hole. He was the rabbit. He was a fiddler fox on the banks of a bubbling brook, playing for fish.

He was a tree. He didn't know he was a tree until he heard the other trees talking.

Yes, he heard other trees talking. Their speech isn't like ours, but trees do talk. Trees can communicate with one other when they are hungry through underground networks of fungi. They then share water and nutrients through their root systems. Trees release scents to warn other trees of danger.

Acacia trees warn each other of approaching giraffe in this way[1].

Ordinary trees communicates without words. Trees in a fairytale forest use words. They converse high above the forest floor. Their vocal chords are the wind-rustled leaves. They talk of weather and woodpeckers, of life and death. They are sentinels of philosophy and photosynthesis.

"Where has the time gone?" Silas heard himself ask them.

The trees had been chattering, but fell silent.

"Time has not gone anywhere," spoke one tree. "It is within us all, in the rings of our trunks. I can feel it. The summer nights. The storms we weathered. The storms we didn't. The winter that froze the forest, when so many splintered and perished. The rumble of men marching to war. The peace at their never returning."

Silas stood there, the tree he was, in contemplation of his own rings.

"There is time within you," continued the tree. "We have lines in our trunks marking the years. You have lines on your face. We grow up. You grow down. We have layers of bark. You have layers of memory."

Silas could feel something within him. Was it time? There were memories, hopes, dreams. Time bound them, but it seemed to him they were not time itself.

"I am in search of a thread," said Silas. "The thread is said to be time. It is woven within the unfading dress of a princess. Have you seen her?"

Those trees were primeval. They remembered the princess and the time before her, before any humans had arrived. The wind rose. The trees waived slowly in it, singing a sad song.

---

1. https://onetreeplanted.org/blogs/stories/how-do-trees-communicate?srsltid=AfmBOoq9Dv_26v9iE2SSV3_tIrkdCx9Zz7EBAcsm-ISmToIZ_KO8j-As

Silas heard the music, but not the lyrics. He'd fallen from the trees into the river. He was a fish. He swam swiftly down the winding, fast-flowing waterway. He sped by the waving, colorful rushes on the riverside. He saw the pale, curious eyes of other fish swimming in his direction. When the river rose he became a kingfisher, soaring into the sky, between the morning and the night. He flew higher and higher until the song and everything else faded away.

The spell the enchanted forest had cast on Silas would also fade away. He returned from the heavens to the heather. He returned to himself. He was whole again. He continued on his way, as though nothing out of the ordinary had happened. He remembered where he was meant to be going, though he had no earthly idea where he was going. Still, he went on with a hopeful heart that led him deeper into those untraveled woods.

After a time, Silas came upon what he thought was a tree of immeasurable girth. He stopped to examine the enormous trunk. He noticed that it was made not of wood, but stone. Looking up, he saw it was no tree at all. It was a lighthouse.

It was towering and tree-colored, thickest at the bottom, narrowing up to the top. At the very top was a brass cupola mantled in sea fog. Candlelit windows dotted the lighthouse. In one, Silas could see a service room. In another a kitchen. There was a spiral staircase. Was someone hurrying down it?

A door opened where there was no door. Silas stepped back. The lighthouse keeper emerged.

"Good gracious!" said the faun, excitedly stroking his horns. "I was not expecting visitors. Come in!"

A Respite from Time

"My name is Deacon. I am the principal lighthouse keeper. Pleased to meet you," the faun extended a bushy hand for Silas to shake, which he did.

Deacon. The name rhymed with that foremost instrument of his occupation—beacon. He looked more ordinary man than mythology. He looked like a lighthouse keeper. Salt-tangled hair hung from his bucket hat. Two stubby horns pointed through the top. Baggy trousers covered his hairy goat legs. Wide, childish eyes betrayed the wrinkles on his face. It was hard to say his age.

"Who are you and what do you do?" asked Deacon.

"Silas is my name. I am a watchman."

"A WATCHMAN!" the faun's eyes widened. "We are in the same line of work! I watch the sea. Tell me, have you ever watched the sea?

"No, I have never seen the sea."

"Follow me. I will show you it to you."

A few words about the lighthouse and its keeper.

Time overtook the village, its fields, the fairytale forest, even the uncrossable sea. But there was one place in those lands that time did not touch—the lighthouse.

It was no ordinary lighthouse. The beacon itself was a navigational aid, though not in the normal, nautical sense. The ordinary lighthouse beacon serves as a navigational aid for ships at sea. There were few ships in those waters. That lighthouse served not maritime pilots, but dreamtime ones. Its function was to protect, guide, and in some cases rescue all those lost dreamers. The beacon marked hazards of the dream seas, subconscious shoals, nightmarish tidal surges, and more. The lighthouse offered safe harbor in the dead of night.

The lighthouse stood upon a rocky promontory between the fairytale forest and uncrossable sea. The body of the tower appeared tree-colored, but was in actuality partially translucent. Looking closely, one could see a service room here, a gallery there, perhaps the keeper hurrying up the spiral staircase or reading within the lantern room. The translucent effect was a result of scattered light fragments from the beacon atop the lighthouse. That beacon was lit by no ordinary flame. The light from it illuminated everything from the darkest depths of the subconscious to the highest heights of dream castle ramparts. Its range and penetration were immeasurable.

The principal lighthouse keeper was like many of that profession, solitary and stoic, a wry smile in the face of a coming storm. There was one habit of the keeper that defended the lighthouse from the onslaught of time. The lighthouse keeper was a musician. Many are. They are musicians, poets and artists. How else to pass the time on those faraway outposts, totally isolated from civilization?

The lighthouse keeper played his fiddle most nights. He never played alone. He was joined by that secret commonwealth of fairies from the fairytale forest, who brought their lutes and lyres. Mermaids often joined them, singing stories from the sea.

Time holds no power over music. A song may be measured in time, but is not meant to be finished in time. It does not lessen or fade with time. Faster songs are not better than slower songs. A piano is meant simply to be played. It is not meant to be hurried, to ensure it complies with the laws of physics. When it comes to music, time is of little consequence.

For the lighthouse keeper, life was music. Music meant here and now, without a nudge from the past or a tug from the future. He would not wait for an imagined tomorrow, never to arrive. He would not work for some treasure, never to be won. He would not wait for life to be lived. He simply lived.

And so time swept by the lighthouse, no more harmful than a passing squall.

Silas followed the faun inside. The moment he entered he felt different. A piping wind whistled through the place like a sentient ensemble. The notes rose and fell, climbing up and down the spiral stairs leading to the topmost platform. Silas listened to the curious music and felt how he once did, before the incursion of time.

"Mind the steps," warned Deacon.

They started up the spiral staircase which ran along the damp, stony walls of the tower. It wound round and round, like some never-ending nautilus shell. There was no railing, so Silas kept as near to the wall as possible. After spiraling up only a few stories, he started to feel queasy. Not so much from walking in circles, but from the wind. It swayed the lighthouse. Silas worried the whole tower might topple over and into the sea.

They reached a platform with a ladder leading up through

a hatch to the top of lighthouse. Silas followed Deacon through. Rising onto the platform and peering over the sea, Silas could hardly believe his eyes. It's one thing to look upon the sea for the first time. It's another to look upon it from such a great height. It looked imaginary. The waves were incantations. They rose and fell, making the waters look like a series of shifting, paint-splattered hills.

How long Silas stood there staring is hard to say because time held no dominion over the lighthouse. When Deacon did finally interrupt Silas, the scene had changed. The sky had darkened. The wind had grown cold. The lantern light burned bright.

"Supper!" Deacon announced.

He led Silas some way down the spiral stairs to a door. It seemed to Silas the door could lead to nowhere but the exterior of the lighthouse. Somehow, it led to a small dining room, warmed by an already burning fireplace.

Fauns are hospitable creatures. Deacon quickly set a table for two near a porthole with a majestic view of the sea. There was white wine and white fish. Silas did most of the eating and drinking. Deacon did most of the talking. He told tales of the sea.

"Is it lonely, being a lighthouse keeper?" Silas asked.

"Not at all. I have friends in the forest. You will meet them tonight. They visit often. The city dweller is more lonely than I. He has too many neighbors to truly know."

"Tell me, have you ever seen a mermaid?"

"Seen hundreds. Kissed one. Far too briny for my liking."

Silas gazed out to sea. He longed to sail upon it, to kiss a mermaid.

"Not all that comes from the sea is amethyst and pearl," said the faun. "Let me tell you a tale."

The faun brought forth fresh wine for the story. Wine is good for stories.

"Once, there was a ship. Now, I have seen all manner of ships. Fishing vessels, ferries, warships. Ships from faraway. Ships of fools. One evening, off in the distance I saw a ship I'd never seen before. It was sailing amidst a terrible storm. It soon wrecked upon my shores."

"It crashed in the dead of night. I rushed down to look for survivors. There was no sign of anyone, dead or alive. You see, it was a ghost ship."

"What does such a ship look like?"

"Couldn't say. It was wrecked when I found it. The ghosts scattered into the woods, haunting them for a while. I dared not venture out after dark for a time."

Silas looked out the window, half-expecting to see a ghost looking back. The waters were calm, a perfect mirror for the stars. Had he not known better, he'd have mistaken the sea itself for another night sky.

"What happened to them?" Silas asked.

"What happened to who?"

"The ghosts?"

"They were seafaring ghosts, the sprits of drowned sailors. I expect they set back out to sea."

A wintry wind blew in from the window. The pair moved their chairs nearer to the fire. Silas noticed a fairy, no larger than a mouse, on the mantel above the fireplace. It had been sleeping. The fairy awoke with a yawn and stretch of its wings. It then began playing a flute.

The faun joined in with his fiddle. Then the sea joined in. Waves crashed like almighty cymbals into the base of the lighthouse. The wind sang a sea shanty. It was a quartet unlike anything Silas had ever heard or seen.

Silas drank and listened to the strange lullabies. Firelight shone upon his travel-worn eyelids. He closed his eyes and imagined himself a mariner, far upon the open sea, with no sight or memory of land. Soon, he was fast asleep, sailing the dream-seas.

Later that night, Silas was startled awake by the crash of a great wave. The lighthouse quivered. Silas quivered with it. He found himself in a straw bed within a small, lantern-lit room at the base of the lighthouse. He tried to go back to sleep but couldn't. The sea was roaring. He must see it for himself.

Silas took the lantern and made his way up the spiral stairs to the top of the lighthouse. He stepped carefully and quietly, so as not to wake the lighthouse keeper, who he assumed to be asleep.

Things were calmer at the top of the lighthouse. The beacon shown with the strength of a star. The wind seemed to have settled down, but not the sea. It was filled with dreams. In the waters, free from norms and tradition, dreamers were transformed into their true, romantic selves. They were water sprites, sea serpents and sailors. They were mermaids, long suffocated on dry land, set free in the dead of night, drunker on water than was possible on wine. They were wild animals, without a yesterday or tomorrow, without a single regret or worry for one of the few times in their lives. Splashes and waves transformed into the tentacles of some monstrous kraken, breaking harmlessly on the bare shoulders of skinny dippers, who danced and sang like sirens. There in the sea they were all mad with possibility and passion. All Silas could hear from the top of his lighthouse were breakers and laughter.

"Evening," a voice startled him from behind. It was the lighthouse keeper.

"Couldn't sleep?"

"Yes. No, I mean. The sea woke me."

"The dreams are restless tonight."

Deacon fidgeted with the beacon.

"Must you tend the light all through the night?" Silas asked. "When do you rest?"

"Yes, this is the life of a lighthouse keeper. I rest when the sea does."

Silas stood there awhile, watching the sea.

"Tell me, do you see any trace of time out there?" he asked.

The faun thought a moment, then stepped out from behind the beacon.

"Oh, it's out there somewhere. The sea is all-consuming. Within it are ages upon ages. Venture far enough out to sea and you'll happen upon eternity."

"Goodnight, lighthouse keeper."

"Goodnight, watchman."

~

Time had stopped altogether in the lighthouse, but back in the village it passed just the same.

That afternoon was a quiet one in the tavern with no name. A few of the regulars made small talk at the bar. The fisherman was one of them. He generally arrived at the bar in the early afternoon, after a day of "work" on the riverside.

"Were the fish biting today?" asked the barkeep to the fisherman. The barkeep knew the answer to the question. So did everyone else. The answer was always the same, more or less. Still, he asked the question.

"Biting?" the fisherman replied. "Biting is an insufficient characterization for what occurred upon the riverside today. Devouring would be a more accurate depiction of the behavior of the fish on this day."

The fisherman was no good at fishing. This was a widely known fact. No one had ever seen him catch a fish and no evidence of a caught fish was ever produced. But like most fishermen, he lied. Every afternoon he arrived at the tavern with some miraculous, fishy tale.

"Devouring?" smirked the knowing cobbler. "Must have been a fish of mythic proportions."

"Truly," the fisherman said. "T'was more serpent than salmon."

"Truly?" the lamplighter egged him on.

"I swear it. The creature was nearly as wide as the river itself. Chewed the hook to tin shavings. Would have chewed me up, had I not clubbed the thing senseless. I nearly died!"

"What became of the monstrosity?" the lamplighter asked.

"I let it go. What would I have done with such a haul? Only catch what you can eat, so they say. I'm certain it swam straight back to the flaming tributaries of hell from whence it came."

All at the tavern shook their head in agreement, none believing any of the story whatsoever. None held the lie against him. That is simply what fishermen do. They lie.

The fabricated tales from the fisherman were not the only cyclical feature of time within the village. The sun rose and fell each day, followed by the moon and stars. The seasons changed, then changed back. Plants rose and fell, then rose again. Animals lived and died, then were born again.

Some of the villagers viewed the cyclical nature of time as suspicious. They cited it as evidence for the non-existence of time. If nothing ever really changed, was time truly passing? The subject was one of those deeply philosophical ones, perfectly suited for the tavern.

It was a shivering, soaking night, the perfect sort to be sheltered from within a tavern. Drinkers drank and watched the raindrops, visible only within the orbit of lantern light outside, or when they came splattering upon the window. The occasional villager splashed hurriedly by, hunched under an umbrella.

The Strange Story of the Man Who Murdered Time

"It has been raining for so long I could not honestly say when it began," observed the barkeep.

"Yes," agreed the damp lamplighter. "It's showing no signs of stopping."

"Perhaps, it will rain forever..."

"Impossible. Time is a straight line," explained the poet. "It goes one way, to one destination—the grave. The rain will end, along with you and I and everyone else. Live life while you have it gentlemen, there is no getting it back once it is gone."

"I respectfully disagree," said the farmer. "The way I see it, time is not a straight line. It is a circle. Planting, growing, harvesting. The day. The night. The sun. The rain. Everything that has happened or will happen will happen again, and again after that."

"I say time is shapeless," said the cobbler. "Indeed, I think it may not exist at all. Nothing ever changes in this village. If it does, you hardly notice."

Most agreed with the cobbler. It is true that time passes slowly in a small town. Only the most watchful notice it.

"What if there are different shapes of time, each unique to the individual?" theorized the blacksmith.

"To ascertain the shape of time with utmost certainty," said the barkeep, "one must know where it starts, and where it ends."

"Where did it start? Where does it end? Why does it end?" they wondered.

"As I said, it starts at birth and ends at death," reiterated the poet. "From one oblivion to the next."

"Time is one straight line, you say?" questioned the miller, who preferred less abstract debates. Like many in town, he generally avoided the subject of time altogether.

"One straight line."

"If time were a straight line, I should like to walk backwards along it to the start of this conversation, to prevent it from ever

happening. I will take my next increment of time in the shape of a glass filled with beer."

The discussion reverted to the usual small town chatter, mostly of weather and gossip. The night passed cold and rainy outside, but warm within. The fireplace crackled and popped, burning that ageless scent. Drinkers cozied up to the snug bar glowing faintly from the firelight dancing in the mirror behind it. Friends crowded around candlelit tables. None took any further heed of time or tomorrow.

Still, tomorrow came. And the day after, and the day after that. Soon, it was another quiet afternoon at the tavern. A few of the regulars made small talk at the bar. The fisherman was one of them.

"Were the fish biting today?" asked the barkeep. The barkeep knew the answer to the question. So did everyone else. The answer was always the same, more or less. Still, he asked the question.

"Biting?" the fisherman replied. "What bit today was no fish. What bit today was a vampiric emanation from the deepest and darkest lagoons of the underworld. Ate me whole, it did. Had to cut my way out with a fishing knife…"

Time is a Sail

Silas stayed as a guest at the lighthouse for a time. It is impossible to say how long "a time" was, or if time passed at all. The lighthouse was a void in time.

The nights passed like a dream for Silas, though he remained awake. He worked nights, becoming a sort of apprentice lighthouse keeper. His day started at dusk, the plunging of the sun into the sea his call to duty. His first duty was to the light. Polish it. Fuel it. Spark it.

Before his nightly watch set in, there was more work to be done. Something always needed an oiling or a painting. A lighthouse keeper passes lifetimes oiling and painting. Then there was supper followed by tea. A lighthouse keeper always has a potent tea on hand—sustenance for the long and lonely watch.

The watch was a meditative ritual, well suited for Silas's reserved and watchful disposition. That sea was worth watching. Remember, it was a dream sea. There were kelpie, kraken, and more fascinating creatures. Time sailed by with the wind. Silas thought he saw it once or twice—a lone and distant sail. Time dared not come near to that citadel of timelessness.

Silas dined and drank with the lighthouse keeper. He would tell stories of life on land, of werewolves and wolpertingers. Deacon would tell stories of the sea, of serpents and Scylla. Music was everywhere in that place. After they'd finished talking they started singing. They sang sea shanties of shipboard tasks, of hauling anchor and heaving the capstan, of sirens singing and hydras howling. The waves rose and the wind whistled along with them.

One evening, Silas asked Deacon about time and that dress worn by the fabled princess.

"Princess?" the lighthouse keeper seemed surprised. "The era of kings and queens passed here long before you. I saw them. They built great fortresses, taller even than the tallest trees. Taller even than this place."

"Was there not an enchanted princess?" Silas asked. "One that wore a dress woven with the fabric of time itself?"

"There were countless princesses, each enchanted in her own way."

"This particular princess is said to have been taken captive by a serpent."

The lighthouse keeper thought to himself. He thought back and back, to a bygone age. He recalled the vast funeral procession of a princess. There were endless lines of knights in long, glimmering hauberks, hands clasped together in prayer to long-forgotten gods. There were chanting maidens, clad in colors of the forest. There were priests with scarlet banners. There was an ancient, sobbing king.

"There was one particular princess," said the lighthouse keeper. "She was lost, long ago. You hope to find her?"

"I hope to save her and the rest of us, from time itself."

"The pursuit of a vanished princess is the pursuit of dreams. It is there you'll find the time you're seeking."

"Where is that?" asked Silas.

"The sea, of course. That is where dreams are. If time is anywhere, it is there."

"I am no sailor," said Silas.

"We will make you one."

So, Silas remained at the lighthouse. He performed his duty to the light at night. During the day, he learned to sail. He helmed the lighthouse dinghy, its sail no bigger than a bath towel. In no time at all (because there was no time in that tower) he was a capable seaman.

Silas was about ready to set forth on the next stage of his unusual adventure, when the weather turned. A storm was approaching, and not just any storm. It was one of those epic, tempestuous upheavals told in tales from long ago, for which there is no safe harbor.

Silas had been sleeping when it arrived. It was not the waves or wind which woke him, but the foghorn. The foghorn did not sound like a foghorn. It sounded like a French horn. No, an orchestra of French horns. They made a noise that was more alluring than alarming.

Silas peered through his porthole. The sea was alive. It laid siege to the lighthouse. Row after row of waves crashed into the stone like legions of blue-coated, crest-crowned warriors. Each time they struck, it was as though a battering ram had crashed into the lighthouse.

Silas hurried from his room. An apprentice lighthouse keeper's duties are most important in a storm. Those duties are to the light, to ensure it remains operational. Without lighthouse lights, ships and dreamers cannot navigate such treacherous seas.

Silas started up the spiral staircase leading up and along the walls of the tower. The going was slow. The wind shook the lighthouse with tremendous force. It seemed at any moment the whole tower might tumble over and crash into the sea.

Silas reached the topmost platform. The swells had risen to an unimaginable height. The tips of the tallest waves splashed over the rails. Cross-winds crossed. It was totally dark, except for the occasional lightning strike. It was totally dark because the beacon was unlit. The beacon was never unlit.

Deacon was at the light. He tried in vain to spark it. The wind and rain were too strong. Silas joined the faun under the cupola. He stood over the lighthouse keeper, blocking the elements to help ignite the beacon. They failed over and over again. It was too wet and windy.

Deacon sent his apprentice to retrieve dry towels from below the top deck. Silas started in that general direction, but would not make it far. A sudden, violent gust of wind sent him soaring over the deck railing.

Silas was too surprised to scream. He plunged head first, straight down toward certain death below. Looking down, trying to ascertain where exactly he might land, the water appeared somehow different. It looked like a withered hedge maze. He'd soon be lost within it.

Lost at sea.

Time is a Mirage

Silas was in mid-air, having been swept from the top of the lighthouse during the storm. The time between his being blown from the lighthouse and splashing into the sea seemed very long. It seemed almost as long as the lifespan of the universe. That span of time was easy to judge because Silas saw it all, from the Big Bang to the end of time itself.

He was billions of years in the past. There was no space or light. Then came the dawn of everything. It looked like a lonesome candle amidst a winter's night. The flicker exploded into an inferno that would become the universe. Masses of stars and galaxies were unfurled like a sail in the wind. He saw his own life pass him by in the blink of an eye. He saw the end of existence itself, of the candle burning out and a return to eternal night.

Then, he struck the sea.

His ordeal in the water was short. There is little to tell of it. He rose and fell with the mountainous swells, carried further and further out to sea. He hardly struggled. There was no point. He was tossed about like a scrap of sea debris. He was pulled under the waves. His lungs filled with foam and brine. His eyes shut. The sea claimed him. His soul left him.

He was dead.

We all wonder what, if anything occurs after death. Many say nothing. Others say something. Some say there is no experience of nothing, so there must be something. Something did happen to Silas. Something strange.

Silas woke to the sound of breaking waves. They weren't the violent waves he'd drowned in. They were peaceful waves, hardly more than ripples in the sea. He could hear a fiddle in the distance, strumming over them.

Opening his eyes, he found himself laying at the end of a long pier. Rising to his feet, he felt lighter. That made sense. After all, he was dead. His body was somewhere in the sea. His spirit was all that remained. The common spirit is no heavier than a dandelion. He was not yet certain he was a spirit, but he suspected it.

The pier led to an island paradise. The sky was clear. The sun shone. The breeze soothed. Palm trees swayed here and there and all around, dancing with the wind as if it were their purpose in life.

There was a canteen. That was where the fiddle strummed. The canteen was on the beach, just beyond the pier. Sailors whored. Dancers danced. Musicians played. None grew tired or bored. The song and laughter was incessant. Silas wanted to be there. He wanted to be with them and one of them, whatever they were.

A slender, somber-looking man stood between the pier and the canteen. He wore a peaked cap and frock coat. He held a scroll. He was the only sober sailor in sight.

"Welcome," he said.

"Welcome where, exactly?" asked Silas.

"Haven't you guessed?" the man raised an eyebrow. "You are dead. That much is clear."

"Dead?"

"You are dead, as I and all the rest on this godforsaken isle."

"But I am here, in the flesh," said Silas.

"I assure you, sir, that you are everlastingly dead. The 'I' that is here is only your apparition," the man explained. "The 'I' that was your flesh and bones is very likely decomposing on the sea floor."

Silas stood there blinking stupidly. He wasn't sad or afraid. Being dead was something and that was better than nothing.

"This is Fiddler's Green," explained the man. "Here is a land of eternal dance and drink for worthy, seafaring souls. I am the warden. Your name, sir?"

"Silas."

"Silas, Silas..." the man murmured to himself as he peered through the scroll. "No record of a Silas. Were you lost at sea?"

"I was."

"Strange," said the warden. "Answer me this. If you found yourself sailing west, and the wind was coming from the west, what point of sail would you be on?"

This was a trick question, one that only a sailor would know. The answer was "in irons," which meant that the boat was sailing directly into the wind, so could not travel forward.

"I... I couldn't say," answered Silas. "I died by the sea, but did not sail much upon it. I was a watchman for most of my days. I only lived by the sea for a time, in the service of a lighthouse keeper."

The music stopped. The canteen quieted. The dancers stood still. Drinkers suddenly appeared sober. They all stared curiously at Silas.

"There is a reason you are not on this list," said the

warden. "No expeditions. No ship logs. You are not listed as a sailor because you are not a sailor. This place is for those who braved the sea, not simply drowned in it. What shall we do with you?"

A sailor stepped forward from the canteen.

"It is true he never sailed the sea, but he stood watch. Many a sailor was saved from a watery grave by the grace of that everlasting beacon."

"Here, here!" cheers sounded from the canteen. The music began again.

Silas and the warden stood staring at one another, wondering what to do.

"There is nowhere to send you but back," said the warden. "Follow me."

The two made their way back to the end of the pier.

"Before I go, might I ask you a question?" asked Silas.

"Certainly."

"Do you know where I might find time?"

"Time? Time is a mirage," said the warden. "Sailors mistake the rolling waves, rounding stars, and veering winds for time passing. What they call the passing of time I call an observation. There is no harm in observing what you call the passing of time, but do not pursue it. Do not mistake it for reality. The pursuit of a mirage is the pursuit of madness. Many a sailor has been lost at sea chasing such visions. Mirages like time are meant to be sailed by and looked upon. Nothing more."

They shook hands and Silas remembered nothing more.

~

Silas wasn't the first villager to die.

Back in the Village of Never Was, time kept right on passing. Seasons turned. Once barren fields became overgrown. Businesses opened and closed. Paint peeled. People peopled. Villagers lived and died.

It was the dying aspect of time that was most noticeable.

The lamplighter was the first to die. He was struck by lightning. The lamplighter worked outdoors, during storms, very near to tall, electrically conductive poles. So, it should not have been such a shock to the town, but it was. He'd been killed. No one had ever been killed before.

The suddenness of his death was disturbing. Had the old-as-the-hills letter carrier died, few would have been bothered. The lamplighter was not old. He was there one minute, gone the next. The absolute nature of his demise was hard for the villagers to comprehend.

One night, the subject was discussed in the tavern with no name.

"Poor fellah," said the barkeep.

"They say he was vaporized," said the miller.

"Yes sir," said the old blacksmith. "Nothing left of him but the lantern he carried."

Remember, the blacksmith was like the letter carrier in that time had passed him by more quickly than the rest. It was the routine that did it.

"Lamps won't shine as brightly without him," said the barkeep.

"Lamps won't shine at all," corrected the miller. "The whole thing is hard to make sense of. One minute he's a man. The next he's nothing at all. Can someone explain that to me?"

The poet rose from his chair eager to answer, because that is what poets do. They are the answerers to unanswerable questions.

"Allow me to explain with a brief demonstration," began the poet. "Lightning appears to have been the slayer. It was not. The untimely demise of the lamplighter was perpetrated by time itself. Time is murdering us all this very moment. Barkeep, a glass of beer if you would?"

The tavern quieted for the demonstration. The barkeep filled a tall, narrow glass with a golden brew, topped perfectly to the brim. The poet raised it for all to see.

"This beer is time. Fate has poured you an amount. Some more, some less."

The poet paused as the villagers examined the time in their glasses.

"Behold, my glass is full," the poet continued. "The future and its possibilities are endless. The night is young. I AM YOUNG! I AM EVERLASTINGLY YOUNG!"

The poet closed his eyes, put the glass to his lips and took a hearty swig.

"The first sip. The first kiss. Nothing after compares to it. Life! The majesty of a summer afternoon. The vastness of a starlit evening. The feel of a spring wind. The music to it all."

The poet stood on his chair, drinking again, holding the glass high.

"A toast! To bold adventure, unfaltering love, a potent brew, and a life so full it counts as two. May this beer flow forever. May I live forever. May we all live forever!"

The whole bar drank to that. They drank and laughed and lived. Some emptied their glasses— time gone the fastest for those who lived the fastest.

The poet stepped down from the stool. Little was left in his glass. His tone changed.

"Time has passed and swiftly at that. There is no undrinking it. The glass cannot be refilled. I will sip the remainder of this beer. I will sip it slowly. I will savor it."

The poet took a few more sips from the glass.

"Time tastes worse, with time. It is flat. I like time less, the less there remains. If only I hadn't drunk the fresh parts so suddenly. If only I had realized their greatness."

The poet finished his glass, along with everyone else in the bar.

"My time is up," the poet held up the glass like a memento. "In this glass was the promise of time. I had a time. It was a good time. In this glass I made memories. You were there. She was there. In this glass was a life. It is as forever gone and forgotten as the once crisp, cool beer."

The drinkers looked thoughtfully into their own empty glasses. They wondered about their own time, about their own lives and memories. What would become of them when they were gone? When would each of their glasses be empty?

Before the old blacksmith left the bar much later that night, and after many more glasses of time, he stopped at the door and shouted.

"I WAS ONCE YOUNG! I WAS ONCE EVERLASTINGLY YOUNG!"

Time is at Hand

Silas did not remain dead. No. His spirit rose from the depths, taking flight over the sea. It rejoined his remains on a distant shore. Luckily, he was discovered by the good people of that land. They fed and sheltered him. He was brought thoroughly back to life, his once drowned self a distant memory. Soon he was aboard a skiff, having resumed his search for time.

Silas traveled far and had many more adventures. He found that fabled dragon, or what was left of it. Its bones guarded a castle that needed no guarding. There was no princess there, adorned in the fabric of time. There was no one at all. There were only ghosts.

An apology is owed to those readers hopeful this story would end like all of those other captive-princess fairy stories, where the damsel in distress is rescued by our hero and the dragon is slain. This is not a stock fairytale. The princess did not need saving. She was dead, and unlike Silas, remained so.

Time had come and gone.

Still, the legend told in the forest by the thieves of the princess withstanding time was not entirely untrue. There was an important grain of truth in that legend. The tale of the princess itself had perseveded through the ages. Stories withstand time. In that fact was an important clue as to the whereabouts of the time Silas was searching for.

Search he did. Silas visited distant lands, hoping for further clues as to the whereabouts of time. He visited cities. There were lost cities and hidden cities. There were cities so big they seemed without end. Other cities were too small to see with the naked eye. There were cities in the sky and others below the earth. There were cities of the dead and of those yet to be born. There were cities of memory and those of forgetfulness.

Each city had its own theory on the identify of time. Some said time was an artist, a sculptor of men and mountains. Others said time was a weaver of moments past. The pious claimed time to be a judge. For some, time was a killer. For others, time was a healer.

The whereabouts of time remained elusive, until the day Silas came upon an unusual city. The city was within a realm enclosed not by seas or mountains, but by ideas. It sat a stone's throw away from wakefulness, but not so far from oblivion as one might guess. It stood closer to yesterday than tomorrow, because there is always more of yesterday than tomorrow in dreams. Far more.

It was morning when he first saw the city. It rose with the sun out of a vast plain, as is from nowhere. No roads led to it. No rivers watered it. There were no farms to feed it. The surrounding countryside was barren.

Stranger still, there was no one to be found within the city, though the wayfaring watchman did see signs of life. Vases of fresh flowers lined the streets. The streets themselves looked to have been recently swept. Much of the architecture looked newly built. Candles burned in some of the windows. The city was clearly occupied. Where was everyone?

It was late in the day when Silas finally encountered an old man.

"Pardon me," said Silas. "Do you know where all the people of this city have gone?"

"Where do you think?" the old man asked back. "They are going about their day."

"I see no one going about their day."

"You must be new here. This city is unlike other cities. You see, this is a city of dreams. The citizens go about their day not in this world, but in the dream one. Here, dream is reality. What you call the waking world is considered a hallucination here."

"This here and now, this conversation, is considered to be some fantasy of the mind?" asked Silas.

"Indeed, which is why you'll find so few here. All the happenings of the city occur within the dream of it."

"I am no dreamer."

"Dreaming comes easily here. You look tired. Just ahead you'll find a grove. Sleep there. You'll awaken to a bustling metropolis."

Silas did as he was told. He lay under a sprawling willow, the wind weeping lullabies with its waving of the branches. The song whispered for him to close his tired eyes. He obeyed, and was soon fast asleep.

Silas awoke as one does in dreams, which is to say he had no idea he was dreaming.

He rose, astonished. The city had come to life. Children played in the grove, their laughter sounding from high in the tree branches. Traffic and trade filled the once vacant streets. Music, conversation, and the clamor of civilization echoed all around.

The layout of the dreaming city was similar to its counterpart in the waking world. It was only when one looked closely did the strangeness of the dreaming city become noticeable. Much of the architecture was shaped by imagination instead of physics. Street surfaces rippled like water. Boats floated on them. People walked on them. There were trees of stone and stones of trees. Pillars of wind supported temples of mist. The houses were vibrant, each filled with families and laughter—the dream of what home should be.

But the city was not all pleasant dreams. There were hints of nightmares. Alleyways were so dark they looked like cosmic voids. Dire wolves prowled the plains on the outskirts of town. The city was not all light and color. It was everlasting twilight. The night loomed like a faraway curse.

Silas wandered as one does in a dream. He was in a stupor and only partially conscious. The locals smiled knowingly at him as he staggered through the streets like the town drunk. They'd had visitors before. Few stayed long.

Silas eventually came to his senses and realized he was dreaming. He soon became like everyone else—a lucid dreamer. He then continued his pursuit of time in the city of dreams. He was hopeful he might find time in a place where ideas seemed to come alive.

Silas got to know the townsfolk. Hope and sorrow sat together at the same tavern all day, every day, toasting to the sadness of yesterday and the promise of tomorrow. Wanderlust wandered the wilderness surrounding the town, often disappearing for long stretches of time. Misadventure followed closely behind. Death drove a carriage. Life pushed one. Fate watched and laughed at the absurdity of it all.

Time was nowhere to be found, at first. Nights passed as if they were days and were ingrained in memory. Days passed almost without notice and were as easily forgotten as dreams once were. For Silas, the dominion of dreams soon became more real than the wakeful one.

Silas heard rumors of a resident who knew the whereabouts of time. She was one who could see through time—a fortune teller. He found her in a gypsy caravan nearest to the darkness on the edge of town. She was a withered old crone, the perfect archetype for such a character. Dreams are the province of archetypes, after all.

"Tell me," said Silas. "If you can tell fortunes, where is yours?"

"It is my fortune to tell fortunes, not to hoard them."

"To tell a fortune is to see through time. If you can see time, where is it?"

"Time is everywhere and nowhere. It is written in the stars. It is cultivated from the earth. It is within you and without you. It simply is..."

"I'm seeking a more precise location," said Silas. "If time were here, in this city of dreams, where would it be?"

She gave Silas a knowing, rotten-toothed smile.

"Time is at hand."

"Where?"

"The library."

Time is a Storyteller

The library looked like one of those goblin-ridden gothic cathedrals. The stones were oddly shaped and altogether missing in some places. The mortar was colorfully swirled and smeared in certain spots, like a watercolor. Two tall arched doors of a gleaming wood with golden strap hinges made Silas think there was something important inside, something unexpected. There was.

Silas knew that time was at hand as soon as he walked in. The scent of it was unmistakable. The library reeked of time. Most do. Time has the distinctive odor released from a long-closed book. Go, find *Treasure Island* in your local library. Open it and breathe deeply. That is the scent of time. The scent is the book dying. It consists of a mixture of organic compounds released as the paper decomposes[1].

At first glance, the inside of the library appeared more normal than the outside. There were long, winding aisles of books. The shelves were so high it was difficult to see beyond

---

1. https://www.sciencehistory.org/stories/magazine/whats-that-smell-youre-reading/

them, to guess the size of the place. It was difficult to see very far in any direction at all. The library was dimly lit by wrought iron candle chandeliers dangling from the arched ceilings high above.

The place was quiet, even for a library. It was quiet because no one was there. Why? Few read in dreams. Fewer visit the library. That is a shame. Dream libraries are worth the visit.

Although there was no one to be seen, Silas sensed a presence. There must be someone, somewhere. A stocker of shelves. A lighter of lights. A reader. A writer.

Silas began his search down one of the meandering aisles. He looked an ordinary library-goer. He strolled, studying the shelves, stopping here or there to browse titles. He stopped often, because the books were unlike any he'd ever seen.

Some of the books were beautifully bound, yet filled with blank pages. Others were unbound, yet beautifully written. Books that seemed normal were not. Letters changed mid-story. Words danced on pages. One aisle of books had faces and voices. They read their stories aloud when he passed. One book read the reader. There were books of memories so dense with moments that they couldn't be moved. There were books of matches and books of bets. There were books of absolutely nothing pretending to be books of absolutely everything.

Silas wandered deep into the library. He read many of the mysterious titles, becoming lost in their pages. Then, he became altogether lost. The library was an impossibly knotted tangle of tales. It contained every book ever imagined and more. Silas had wandered too far within it.

Silas roamed the library for what seemed like days. He traveled to strange sections, where the aisles began to look like the stories within the books themselves. Rows of shelves turned to hedgerows. The eyes of fairies and gnomes peered curiously at him from the shrubs. One aisle was so flooded it looked like a creek. The waters were clearer than a magic mirror. Another aisle contained teeth instead of books, like the throat of an immense dragon. Silas avoided these sections, for fear of becoming even more lost, or worse.

He'd been walking down one aisle which was so long, that after a while he became convinced it would never end. He may have been right, but would never know for certain, because he never made it to the end. He stopped when he saw something ahead.

It was a dark shape, resembling a man with his back turned. As Silas stared, the figure lifted its head and turned slowly around. It was aware of him. It stared at Silas for a few long seconds, head tilting with interest. Silas stared back.

Silas walked nearer to what he guessed to be a man. It was no man. It was a shadow. Candlelight avoided the thing. Hardly any of it could be seen. Gleaming eyes of emerald were all the light it shed. They drifted ominously through the library like will-o'-wisps. When the shadow browsed the shelves, it stained the books an inky black. Silas's heart darkened the nearer he drew to the figure. Still, he found himself drawn to it.

He was drawn to it because it was time. Its inconceivability gave it away.

Sword drawn, Silas crept nearer to that thing he'd hunted for so long. As he did, it began to grow taller. Soon, it was a towering phantom, high as the ceiling. Its dark hand reached down toward the terror-stricken Silas. He turned to run. Time howled as it gave chase. It sounded like the chime of the grandest of grandfather clocks.

It was a straight and strange race down the never-ending aisle. There was nowhere to turn or hide. The pursuit entertained many of the onlooking books. They roared as the pair rushed by, as if it were some sport. Silas was fast, but time was faster. Silas could hear time gaining on him, its tick-tock heartbeat piercing the silence of the library.

Time would catch Silas, that much was clear. Its shadow was all-encompassing, its presence one of inevitability. Just before it caught him, the aisle sloped sharply downward. Silas tripped on a stray book. The book was one of those unreadable, self-aggrandizing memoirs which, having never been read, had mutinied from the shelf. Silas tumbled forward over the book. He lay helpless in the aisle.

And just like that, time passed him by.

It isn't such a strange a thing for time to pass so swiftly. What child hasn't passed a summer in the blink of an eye? What parent hasn't looked at that same child and thought, "Where have the summers gone?" Who among us will not someday linger in front of the mirror, worn and withered, wondering at the ruthlessness of time's progression?

Silas felt the passage of time in an instant. His back hunched. His bones ached. His strength left him. His hair thinned, turning from straw to silver. He felt less alive. He felt *tired*.

He lay there in that peculiar state of consciousness between the dreaming and awakening. His heart thumped with a terrifying ferocity, but not for long. The threat of time had passed. He looked around at the stillness of that library of dreams, and realized it was just that—a dream.

Time was there. It had shrunk again to the size and shape of a man. It looked not at all dangerous. It looked like a librarian. Time was climbing a ladder, shelving books.

"Who are you?" asked Silas.

"Don't you know?" responded time. The voice was owlish. It echoed throughout the library. "I am that which you have pursued for so long. I am time."

Silas realized then that he the hunter had become the

hunted. He'd pursued that elusive foe for a lifetime, only to have been overtaken by it in an instant. He wondered what everyone wonders about time. How had it bested him? Where had it gone?

"It was amusing, chasing you as you chased me," explained time. "You nearly had me, once or twice. I was in the river, just not where you leapt in. I was the source. I was the uncatchable thief. I brushed past you with a grin, stealing so much of yesterday you hardly noticed it was gone. I do keep a fabric. So do you. It is a patchwork quilt of memory. I waited for you outside the lighthouse. I waited and waited. None are more patient than I. I will get that lighthouse keeper, someday. I lost you that day of the storm, but you turned up again. I knew you would. I didn't think I'd find you here, yet here we are."

"You don't appear to be a river, thief, or quilt. What *are* you?" asked Silas.

"I am a storyteller. Why else would I be in the library?"

Time climbed down from his ladder and came closer to Silas. His eyes were unblinking and all-seeing. Silas found it difficult to face them. They contained the history of everything. Silas wondered how much of history had passed him by on his quest.

His quest. He must finish it.

"I've come here to kill you," said Silas.

"I cannot be slain, not in the way you mean. And even if I could, what good would that do you? What would you do without me?"

"I would do as I always did. Things would go back to the way they were. There would be no misfortune. No death or destruction. The days would pass without change, without sadness."

"There is a story in this library where nothing changes. No one reads it."

"I'm not here to tell stories. I'm here to murder you."

"That *is* a story, and a strange one at that!" laughed time. "You should be thanking me, not murdering me. Without me, you would still be watching the nothingness of night in the Village of Never Was. Without me you would have no purpose, no past or future. All those songs you heard in the lighthouse—they are immune from time, yet depend upon it. A song without time is simply noise. I am the melody. I am the rhythm of song, of life. Without me, you would be meaningless, storyless."

"I regret having not already murdered you," said Silas. "I'm certain this feeling of regret won't last long, because without time there is no such thing as regret."

Silas tried to draw his sword but failed. He failed again and again. The sword was too heavy. He looked at his aged hands, blotchy and wrinkled. He felt his scraggly arms. He hardly had the strength to clench his own fists.

"One moment," said time. "I may be able to help you succeed in your quest after all."

Time turned and walked further down the aisle. He perused the shelves, looking for a title.

He pulled a book from the shelf. It was a small and unassuming book, much like this one.

Very much like this one.

"You say you're here to kill time? There is nothing like a book for such a quest. Here, read this one. You will find it interesting. It is the story of your life. Few tales kill as much time."

Time handed the book to Silas. The title read:

The Strange Story of the Man Who Murdered Time

Silas began reading.

. . .

The Strange Story of the Man Who Murdered Time

Once upon a time, there was no time. At least, not in one peculiar village. The village did not drift with those doom-currents down the river of time. It sat safe and sound on the water's edge. Because of its location, the village was not behind the times or ahead of the times. It was entirely outside of time.

Silas soon lost himself in the story. He'd vanquished time at last.

The Village That Always Was

As for The Village of Never Was, time summarily conquered it.

Time possessed the town so thoroughly, the townsfolk became obsessed with it. They built an immense clocktower in the center of town as if in worship of it. They wore time on their wrists. They carried it in their pockets. They abided by and obeyed time, as though it were God.

Time changed the town, mostly for the worse. Its culture and architecture eroded with the advent of technology. Its people and industries were exploited by outsiders. Progress and productivity became more important than people. People complied with the new reality. Happiness became an elusive destination, as opposed to an everyday reality.

The healing and forgetful nature of time were its only redeeming qualities. After a while, the Village of Never Was and its timeless grace were forgotten. The town was renamed Fairview, Franklin, or Fort something or other. Time was assumed to have always been there—the Village That Always Was.

The villagers changed with the times. They didn't walk.

They rushed. They didn't rest. They worked. They worked to exhaustion and deadlines. They didn't breathe. They deliberated and schemed. They stopped looking up at constellations of stars and instead looked down at ledgers of accounts.

Except for the poet. The poet never stopped being a poet. Few do. Poets and artists that stop being poets and artists wither away like flowers in the dark.

Time had its way with the rest of the townsfolk. The lovers fell out of love, then back into it. The blacksmith became a clocksmith. The farmer became a mechanical engineer. The mechanical engineer became a software engineer. Time will tell what becomes of the software engineer.

Time was scarce. People coveted it. Many mistakenly believed that time *was* money. They thought more time could be gained through the hoarding of treasure. In actuality, the pursuit of wealth destroyed time. Sadly, many townsfolk wasted their lives in such senseless pursuits.

Certain parts of the town were less disturbed by time. The tavern is still there. These days, it pours more memories than hopes or dreams. Time still isn't tracked there. The patrons haven't changed much. Go there. You'll find the fisherman telling tall tales. You'll hear the same pontificating over the meaning of life. And someone will be very, very drunk.

Time would eventually breach the dream-seeing lighthouse. No one knows what became of the faun lighthouse keeper, or any other lighthouse keeper. They are no more. Sadly, lighthouse keepers have been replaced by machines. Moonlit nights have been replaced with electric lights. The stars have all but vanished. The insides of a lighthouse are filled not with music and conversation, but with the low, monotonous drone of engines.

As for Silas, he remained in that faraway city of dreams.

He found a job there. Watchman. He was well qualified. He wandered the lanes of water beneath the lamps of twilight. He granted safe passage to pleasant dreams. He kept nightmares at bay. He befriended others like him—wandering spirits with no interest in that other world and its worship of time.

Silas dreamed himself a little house by the sea. The waters were filled with memories. There were owls and otters, bands of thieves, fauns and Fiddler's Green. There was the Village of Never Was. There was the young man he once was.

More time passed. The sea filled with more memories.

But those memories faded, along with the city of dreams itself. Its residents died or awoke and were not replaced. Dreamers have all but vanished from this rational age. Fantasy is frowned upon. Imagination is ignored. What is a dream these days but a senseless clumping together of the day's events?

Silas visited the library on occasion. He never encountered time again. It had passed. He did rediscover his story. This story. He read it often. He read it to relive those times that had been lost, to vanquish time once more. He vanquished it word by word, time and time again.

Silas read until he could read no longer, until his story was truly at an end. He then passed back into that inexplicable realm of timelessness—the same place from which we've all come and shall, at our own story's end, return.

Author's Note

I hope you liked reading this one. For a very little book, it took a very long time to write. Having finally finished it, I feel like a mass murderer of time. I hope that my next book doesn't take so long to get into the hands of readers.

If you enjoyed the book, please leave a review. I'm an independent author, with no marketing or public relations support from a traditional publisher. Reviews are important in helping to connect me with readers like you.

If you'd like to check out other books I've written, or receive future notifications of upcoming titles, subscribe to my mailing list at https://www.absurdistfiction.com/. You can also get those updates by following me on Amazon here: Author Page

I've borrowed enough of your time. Thanks for lending it.

Until next time.

STEVE WILEY, AUTHOR

Steve is a purveyor of the finest in speculative literature from Chicago. He has authored six novels, and his short fiction has been published everywhere from *Crannóg* magazine in Galway, Ireland, to *Papercuts* magazine in Pakistan. Steve once passionately kissed a bronze seahorse in the middle of Buckingham Fountain. Seriously, he did.

For new title release and other information, visit Steve's author website at https://www.absurdistfiction.com/ , or follow him on Amazon Here.

You can email Steve at lavenderlinepress@gmail.com.

Work Cited

Bischoff, Manon, and Jeanna Bryner. "Evidence of 'Negative Time' Found in Quantum Physics Experiment." *Scientific American*, 30 Sept. 2024, www.scientificamerican.com/article/evidence-of-negative-time-found-in-quantum-physics-experiment/. Accessed 27 Aug. 2025.

Weeden, Meaghan. "How Do Trees Communicate?" *One Tree Planted*, 6 Mar. 2025, onetreeplanted.org/blogs/stories/how-do-trees-communicate?srsltid=AfmBOopZ9o4e6O3p4pwlB5kXGa4dpljPUvquTpJ_u-KQm456FlGAAt9tq. Accessed 27 Aug. 2025.

Wiener, Ann Elizabeth. "What's That Smell You're Reading?" *Science History Institute*, 26 Mar. 2018, www.sciencehistory.org/stories/magazine/whats-that-smell-youre-reading/. Accessed 27 Aug. 2025.

www.ingramcontent.com/pod-product-compliance
Lightning Source LLC
LaVergne TN
LVHW020115280426
837388LV00064B/8